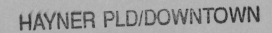

✓ W9-ADG-695

MAY 2 7 2014

R E C E I V E D
MAY 2 7 2014
By_____

HAYNER PUBLIC LIBRARY DISTRICT
ALTON, ILLINOIS

OVERDUES 10 PER DAY, MAXIMUM FINE
COST OF ITEM
ADDITIONAL $5.00 SERVICE CHARGE
APPLIED TO
LOST OR DAMAGED ITEMS

HAYNER PLD/DOWNTOWN

Washday

by **Eve Bunting**

illustrated by **Brad Sneed**

Holiday House / New York

To Ed, Fred, and John Bunting, in memory of their mother — E. B.

For Emily — B. S.

Text copyright © 2014 by Eve Bunting
Illustrations copyright © 2014 by Brad Sneed
All Rights Reserved
HOLIDAY HOUSE is registered in the U.S. Patent and Trademark Office.
Printed and Bound in November 2013 at Toppan Leefung, DongGuan City, China.
The artwork was created with pencil and watercolor on hot press watercolor paper.
www.holidayhouse.com
First Edition
1 3 5 7 9 10 8 6 4 2

Library of Congress Cataloging-in-Publication Data
Bunting, Eve, 1928-
Washday / by Eve Bunting ; illustrated by Brad Sneed.
— 1st ed.
p. cm.
Summary: One sunny Saturday in 1889, Lizzie helps
her grandmother scrub, boil, rinse, and hang loads of
laundry, although she would rather be having a tea party
with her best friend, Lucy, and their dolls, Amelia Cordelia
and Belinda Lavinia.
ISBN 978-0-8234-2868-7 (hardcover)
[1. Laundry—Fiction. 2. Frontier and pioneer life—Fiction.
3. Grandmothers—Fiction.] I. Sneed, Brad, ill. II. Title.
PZ7.B91527Was 2014
[Fic]—dc23
2012040347

On Saturday I walk to Grandma's house to help
her do the wash. She needs me till Ma can come again.
I've brought Amelia Cordelia, my doll, with me.
I'm not very happy about coming today
because I'm missing our doll tea party.

"I'm sorry," I tell Amelia Cordelia.
"I know you were looking forward to
the party with your friend."

Amelia Cordelia smiles. She
always smiles. She is a very
good-natured doll.

Grandma opens her door and kisses my cheek.
She says hello to Amelia Cordelia.
"How's your ma?" she asks.
"Our baby's coming soon," I say.

The kitchen is full of steam from the copper boiler on the stove. There's a smell of lye soap.

"Are you ready for work, Lizzie girl?" Grandma asks me.

"I am." I set Amelia Cordelia in a kitchen chair and roll up my sleeves.

Shep, Grandma's dog, rises from his warm spot by the stove and hobbles beside us. He's sixteen years old and has the misery in his back.

"It's a good day for the drying," Grandma tells me.

The boiler is simmering. The steam almost suffocates me and makes my eyes water. We shave the bar of lye soap into it. It's miracle soap. It cures poison oak and dandruff and even ringworm. Grandma makes it herself from the beef drippings and the watered ash from her fireplace.

We lift the boiler off the stove. It takes both of us to heft it onto the bench.

"Two strong women," Grandma says.

Before we put in the clothes we sort them in piles on the kitchen table.

The first one has sheets and other whites. I know Grandpa's drawers are hidden among them, but Grandma doesn't let me see them.

Then we make a stack of coloreds and another of britches and rags.

Shep lies close to the stove. "Old bones," Grandma says. Shep never gets in the way or trips us up. He has seen a lot of washdays.

I think about my friend Lucy. She was coming to my house today for our doll tea party. We had a dishcloth over a bale of hay in the barn, and my pink doll tea set with its teeny cups and plates was all ready.

Ma and I had baked snickerdoodles, small so they would fit our plates.

"Stop day dreamin', pet," Grandma says.

I give myself a little shake.

We examine the whites. These are the Sunday go-to-meeting clothes and must be spotless. I find a big brown stain on Grandpa's best shirt and rub it on the washboard. Rub, and rub, and rub. Grandma glances over.

"Molasses," she says. "That man can't get enough of molasses on his bread."

His shirt and her chemise and a cotton blouse have to be boiled.

Next the coloreds get washed. "Take the
britches and the rags out," Grandma says.
"Use the broom handle."

I fish them out and drop them in the
rinse water.

Then we take turns twisting the handle of the wringer and pulling the clothes through the rollers. The wringer makes them flat as flapjacks. They aren't anything till you shake them out and then they're themselves again.

We pin the whites on the line that stretches between the trees and spread the rest on the grass or over the fence.

The whites on the rope dance. The clothes on the grass pull to get free, but the grass won't let go. Mrs. McComber's goat in the next field chews on one of the rags on the hedge.

"No matter," Grandma says. "There's nothing there worth a bent nickel."

We meander back to the house, Shep at our heels.

Grandma rubs her back. "You're a great helper, Lizzie girl," she says. "I do thank you."

Amelia Cordelia and I smile. "You're welcome."

"You deserve a rest," Grandma tells me.

I sit on the porch with a glass of buttermilk, thick and curdy, the way I like it. Amelia Cordelia does not like buttermilk.

Shep slurps on a bone, *slurp*, *slurp*, *slurp*. Inside of me I feel satisfied. Like when I've finished my lessons. The doll tea party drifts into my mind and makes me sad again, but just for a minute.

Shep drops his bone and starts to bark. He rushes into the house and I pay no mind. He must have smelled a squirrel in our backyard. Shep does not allow a squirrel in his territory.

Grandma is gone a long time. When she comes out,
I see she has put on a fresh apron.

"Come in now," she says. "We have company."

When we go in, there is Lucy with Belinda Lavinia.
I am flabbergasted.

"How did you get here?" I ask.

"Your pa walked the both of them over," Grandma
says. "They came in the back way."

"Sit down now, the four of you," Grandma says.

"Oh, Grandma! This is as good as having our tea party in the barn. This is a real grown-up doll tea party."

There are gingersnaps on a plate and roses in a jelly jar in the middle of the table. And tiny snickerdoodles on a yellow plate.

Grandma sees me looking. "Your ma sent the snickerdoodles with your pa," she says.

She brings her teapot and fills our cups with milk and a little tea.

"Pearl tea," I tell Lucy. "My favorite."

I am happy but choked up, the way I get when something is too nice to hold inside.

I pick up the yellow plate.

"Grandma," I say. "I love you.

"Have a snickerdoodle. They're small. Have two."